FRIDAY NIGHT
FOOTBALL MURDER

LOUIS CISNEROS

Order this book online at www.trafford.com
or email orders@trafford.com

Most Trafford titles are also available at major online book retailers.

Print information available on the last page.

ISBN: 978-1-4907-8570-7 (sc)
ISBN: 978-1-4907-8571-4 (hc)
ISBN: 978-1-4907-8577-6 (e)

Library of Congress Control Number: 2017917484

Trafford rev. 11/16/2017

 www.trafford.com
North America & international
toll-free: 1 888 232 4444 (USA & Canada)
fax: 812 355 4082

CHAPTER 1

Day 1

Ring!

Ring!

Ring!

"¡Levantate werka!"

Something moved in between the blankets, and with sleepy eyes said, "¡Ay mami! Welcome to America."

"Oh porque te quieres casar con un gringo."

"¡Ay mami por favor!"

The mother comes back into the room again and takes the blanket off her daughter.

"Mejor que hacer tortillas que pan, ¡si por favor, casate con un mexicano!"

Her daughter angrily responded, "¡Sí mami, voy a casarme con un gringo! Sí, quiero comer pan blanco más que comer tortillas quemadas."

Maria, as one of the cheerleaders at Harbor High, was nervous and excited about the district game. It was a good time for her to impress the gringo boys. "Mami, don't worry about me. *Por favor*, let me get ready for school!"

Ringgggggggggggggggggggggg!

In another part of town . . .

The alarm clock went off, and the music began, but I felt like rolling over and forgetting about teaching today. The weekend had been a total failure. It went by just like it was a few hours ago.

My mouth felt like the 101st Airborne had marched over it and forgotten their officers' latrines. I jumped up and made it to the head where the foul smell of last night's worshipping of the toilet hit me like a howitzer. It turned my gut once more.

I knew I was running late. It was 7:30 a.m. The shower, as usual, was awakening, but the shave irritable. I glanced at the mirror of the man who stood before it—a complete wreck. My eyes had huge bags that could be used by Oscar De La Hoya as speed bags. It wouldn't have made any difference to my face. I was getting old. I looked old and tired.

It was a nice autumn day in Santa Cruz. Tourists walked along the boardwalk, and beachcombers looked for seashells, the cold waves shuddering on their feet. The ocean's thunderous rhythm on the rocks sent water into the air, making millions of rainbows, as the surfers perched on the jetty waiting for the tide to come in, in order to begin a series of wipeouts.

Bewitched by the spectacular view, the ocean seized my mind, and I began to imagine the savage love affair I could have on the wet sand. The sunrise to my right and the misty breeze to my left collided on my face and stopped me from fantasizing. I must concentrate on school and not on that wicked woman. Did I have a lesson plan or was I going to brainstorm? Not fully recovered from my fantasy, I dragged my brain away from her. The drive to the school was short, and I stopped for a cup of joe. The school building was just around the curve. I made it just in time; classes had not resumed.

As I walked toward the classroom, I felt like going back to my car and driving far away. The walls of the school had been defaced over the weekend with graffiti with gang signs. Damn gangsters!

I managed to make through the crowd of students to my classroom. I had to get organized before the animals came in. My mouth still had that sour taste, not to mention the headache that I had. The bell rang before I had a chance to sit down. Oh no! Here they come.

Minutes later . . .

"Please, students, settle down and get ready for the Pledge of Allegiance."

"I pledge allegiance to the flag of the United States of America and to the republic for which it stands, one nation, under God, indivisible, with liberty and justice for all."

"Class, please be seated and turn in your homework so we can begin this morning. We will review the questions you had over the weekend. Also, pass your work folder to the front."

The students, as usual, began to go through their books, making all kinds of racket with the papers.

"Class, can't you be a little less noisy? Please! Okay, let's get the show rolling. Remember, class, that the first question has two parts to it. Also, there isn't a right or wrong answer to the questions because it's philosophical. So any volunteers? Chris, how about you."

Chris O'Connor was a very good-looking boy with long brown hair that matched his eyes. He had just about every girl on the campus creaming to go out with him. He had been chosen most popular by the student body for the past three years. He also made the varsity squad in his sophomore year and became the star quarterback for the school. This boy had the teachers in the palm of his hand. All he had to do was to flex his muscles and flutter his brown eyes. Except for me. I didn't put up with his shit. Big dumb ass!

"Chris, the class is still waiting," I said.

"I don't know, Mr. Perez," he answered.

"Why don't you know, Chris? May I ask, did you do your homework?"

"No, sir, I had football practice."

I was raging. "What does football have to do with the problems in Iraq? Chris, you know we studied all last week about the situation in that country. Is it that you don't care, or is football more important?"

"I was tired from football practice, Mr. Perez," he answered.

The class went into uproarious laughter with Chris's dumb answer.

"Okay, class, who can help Chris with this difficult question?"

By this time, the class was in complete hysteria.

"Vanessa, what did you call the Iraqis?"

She responded, "Muslim baby killers, well, that's what my father calls them. My father said that they go around placing mines on the desert roads where the American servicemen are driving in their Humvees through the desert."

"Vanessa, don't you think that the American servicemen try to kill them too?"

"But that's different," she responded naively.

"Vanessa, there's no difference. They're just as dead," I said to her. "Class, since there are many misconceptions about the war, I will reserve the library all this week so you can read the newspaper or check out books on the Middle East. Also, I want everyone to make a three-page report on the Iraqis. It can be on people, such as President Bush or Saddam Hussein, or the Allies relationship with the Iraqi government. And it's due Friday! That means you too, Chris!"

The students are making faces, those ugly faces like the ones on the dead soldiers.

"Before I dismiss the class, I need to talk to you, Chris. Class, here's your homework on the blackboard. So get to it. Chris, would you please step up to my desk?"

"What do you want to talk to me about, Mr. Perez?" Chris asked.

"It's about you not doing your homework. Also, it's your grades, Chris. You seem tired and troubled, and I'm concerned about it. Is the practice too much for you, or what?"

"No, Mr. Perez," he said very politely.

"Chris, I had a conference with Coach Harris about your grades to see if we can't do something about football practice."

"But, Mr. Perez! We're having our district game this week."

"Yes, Chris, and you have homework this week, so please do it, so we can win the district. Okay?"

The bell rang.

"Class, you're dismissed."

After an ordeal like that with Chris, any teacher might pray for early retirement. But without students like Chris, the teaching profession wouldn't be so rewarding. So another day, another headache in spite of the problems. But drugs . . . that boy is on them, sure as hell. I made my way toward the faculty room where I met Coach Harris.

"Coach Harris, I'd like a word with you."

"Shoot."

Coach Harris stood six-feet-five and was 250 pounds of Texas beef. A former All-American from Stanford, he never made the pros. There were rumors that he had taken some money or made some side bets on some of the games.

"It's about Chris O'Connor," I said as I stood like an ant next to the giant.

"What about Chris?" he asked and turned away from me. It was the beer smell that I still had in my mouth.

"It's his grades. He is not doing very well because of football practice."

He responded, "So what do you want me to do? Tutor him?"

"No, Coach, just have a talk with him so he can graduate. Coach, he needs the credit to finish high school."

"So give it to him."

"You know I can't do that!"

"Well, what the hell do you want me to do with him?" he screamed at me.

"Coach, just have a talk with him. That's all I'm asking."

"Look, bean brain, that's not part of my job. I'm a football coach. Not a damn counselor!"

Out of frustration, I shouted back, "Look, asshole, Chris will have to do his work, even if I have to keep him from the game!"

"What the hell is wrong with you? We need him to quarterback. Without Chris, there isn't a chance to win the district."

"Tough shit!"

"You are a sorry ass!" he shouted and walked off.

Minutes later, I ran across Mr. Nguyen as I was entering my classroom. Mr. Nguyen was the school's principal and had been for the past five years. Before becoming principal, he taught social studies and was a damn good teacher. But now, he sits on his big fat butt and talks to the superintendent about trivialities. What a waste of talent.

"What's this I hear about you keeping Chris from the game?" he asked.

"I see you met with Coach Harris this morning."

"Yes, I did, and he was pretty upset about it. And I don't blame him. What the hell is wrong with you, Steve? Can't you and Coach Harris stop fighting each other and come to a mutual agreement? Why, is it some sort of a Mexican standoff? Steve, come to your senses."

"I don't like the man. He's an egotistical asshole. That's all."

"That's all! The man is an All-American from Stanford University, Steve. Give him some credit."

"The question at hand is about Chris's grade and not Coach Harris's past or future."

He said with a smile, "That's funny, I received some good reports on him just this morning from his teachers."

Holding back my temper, I shouted back, "That's because they're afraid of him. He's a jerk!"

"Aren't you stretching it a bit, Steve?" he said with that stupid smile on his face.

"Hell no! Why was he kicked out of Harbor High School?" I asked.

"He was discharged because of technicality."

"Technicality! Horseshit! He was fired because he was screwing a cheerleader in the boys' locker room," I screamed at this senile fool.

Mr. Nguyen's face was turning super red, like an old chameleon who was camouflaging his big nose from a predator. He was still insisting that this jock was a good model for the students and not accepting my opinion that he was a menace to the school.

"And furthermore, we're winning more games than we ever have before," he said.

I angrily replied, "Yes, we're winning more games, but how are we winning them? By giving the football team drugs. The whole damn school knows about what is going on. Open your damn eyes, Mr. Nguyen."

Mr. Nguyen's face was ready to burst open when he heard what I had said. I could imagine what was going through his mind. Was it true?

"And before I forget, Steve, there will be a special faculty meeting this afternoon about your allegation. Also, Steve, please think about your future. You know that Mr. Murray is retiring this year and the position is open for a person of your—"

As I walked down the empty hallways of the school, I thought I could hear the echoes of the students, but it was only the janitor sweeping the debris from the corners. The ancient man moved very slowly, like he knew every corner of the building. With a faceless expression, he moved the broom with grace and style that would put any housewife to shame.

"Good night, old man. I see business is picking up," I said with a depressing smile on my face. I knew I had to face the faculty. As usual, the old man just continued to sweep the hall without saying a word.

I entered the faculty room. I smelled the smoldering cigarettes and stale coffee and heard the horrifying laughter of Coach Harris.

"Glad you made it, Steve."

The room was very quiet. It suddenly dawned on me that this would be a kangaroo court and that I would be its victim. These damn faceless people.

"Okay, people, let's get this meeting over so we can go home. There have been some complaints and allegations by one of our staff. So let's do it."

CHAPTER 2

Drinking Time

After the faculty meeting, I needed a drink or two to calm my nerves. Those damn hypocrites, they knew that the coach was giving the player drugs. The evening had fallen rapidly. The heavy fog began to drift toward the inland. The cool ocean breeze whirled around the alleys between the apartment complexes in small tornados. A funny thing came to mind: the old man at school. The whirlwinds reminded me of him. Poor bastard, his work is never done.

I fixed me a scotch and water, turned the tube on, and watched the six-o-clock news. This secondhand TV, it takes five minutes to warm up. That's good. It gives me time to fix a second drink.

Peter Jennings was giving brilliant commentary on the Iraqis. As usual, the Iraqis were getting their asses kicked, someplace called Kirkuk. The men from the Seventh Division had sustained severe casualties in the brutal skirmish that had lasted for three days. My god! What the hell is the military doing? Either finish the damn war or bring their boys back. Damn, this news is frustrating; I guess I'll take a drive to the Ideal Bar and Grill. The Ideal Bar and Grill was where the teachers went to unwind.

As soon as I entered the lounge, psychedelic lights came on from a small lighthouse hanging from the middle of the ceiling. These work automatically when one walks in the doorway.

I started toward the bar. The different colors for the lighthouse were moving counterclockwise, and this made the Spanish galleons on the wall seem like they were moving toward the bar, where there was a captain's bell that you rang for service. Abe came over to take my order. Abe, the owner of the lounge, was a retired naval captain. He was a huge man with broad shoulders and a beard that made him look like a bear. Abe was a gentle man for his size, and he was as strong as an ox.

"Scotch and water?" Abe asked.

"Right."

"How was school?" he asked.

"As usual, no penetration."

A smile came over Abe's bearded face, and he said, "Hang in there."

I picked up my drink and walked toward the patio, my usual spot. Here I could stare at the darkness of the ocean and daydream. After a few seconds, a feeling of tranquility came over me as the cold breeze caressed my face. I began to daydream about the woman I was making love to on the beach this morning. Just as I was in conquest of this beautiful creature, I felt someone tapping me on the shoulder. It was Abe. I answered with disgust, "Yes."

"Someone brought you a drink," he replied.

"Oh! Who was so kind?"

"Coach Harris."

"Shit, are you sure it's a drink or is it quinine, Abe?"

A smile came over Abe's big fat face, as he turned and walked away, nodding his head to reassure me that it wasn't poison. I could see Coach Harris walking toward me. He had a huge smile on his face and said, "Hi, turkey!"

"What do you want?" I said nervously.

He answered with a malicious tone in his voice.

"I want you to stop spreading that rumor about me and the damn drugs."

"Those aren't rumors! It's true, and you know it."

"Look, son of a bitch, you can get me in serious trouble!" he shouted.

"I like your vernacular, Coach. Is that what they taught you at Stanford?"

Like a flash of lighting, *wham!* The bastard hit me. Oh my god. What was happening to me? I stumbled on to the floor of the patio. The table went crashing to the floor, the bottles knocking against the wall. I managed to jump up and pick up a chair and *smack!* I hit Coach Harris on the side of the head with it. He screamed out, "You son of a bitch!"

By this time, I was wheezing and gasping for air. Again, I raised the chair that I had broken on

Coach Harris' head. *Wham!* I was hit with a left hook that sent me flying on top of another table, sending glasses filled with bourbon and Coke all over me. He was kicking the shit out of me. His foot felt like a Mack truck when it hit me. The pain was unbelievable. I was coughing and spitting blood. Women were screaming and falling on their asses. Coach Harris was having a field day on my ribs. I managed to pull myself up, trying not to vomit. I staggered down the bar, past the half-drunk nightclubbers, and into the parking lot, wondering if I was missing any teeth.

Shit! There goes my dental bill. As I leaned against my car, I heard someone call my name. Holy shit! Another ass kicking. I jumped into my car and started it. Two figures began to run toward the car. I turned the lights on. If I'm going to get an ass kicking, at least I'll know who they are. Dammit! It's Vanessa and Chris. What the hell are they doing here? They scared the hell out of me!

"Mr. Perez, are you okay?" Vanessa asked with a frightened tone in her voice.

"Yes," I answered with pain that made my upper lip quiver. Vanessa turned away so she did not have to look at my face. Then she said, "Mr. Perez, Coach Harris wants to hurt you."

"I know, Vanessa. He just did a job on my face." Vanessa didn't realize that I was terrified of that maniac. But I kept my composure and said, "Don't worry about me. I can take care of myself."

"Be careful, Mr. Perez."

"You bet."

As they walked off, I reached into my shirt pocket for a cigarette. My lip was still hurting, and the smoke burned it. I threw the cigarette out the window. I looked toward the sky. The moon was surrounded by a circle of fog. The fog had thickened. I decided to go back home like a defeated dog.

I rolled back and forth in my bed, fighting my morning hardness, deciding whether I should call in sick. I could smell the ocean air. I had dreamed about the woman on the beach again last night. I heard a light tap on my door and then three more. I managed to get up and put my robe on. Dammit, my lips and ribs ached. I opened the door, and there stood a tall skinny policeman with a tablet in hand.

"Yes?" I said.

"Good morning. Are you Steve Perez? The owner of the blue Bug, license 534 LC?" he asked.

"Yes, I am," I answered.

"Sir, I have to inform you that your car has been vandalized," he said with a broad smile.

"What! What the hell are you talking about?"

"Sorry, sir."

"But my car is downstairs."

"Yes, I know. But someone has turned it over completely, sir."

"What?" I screamed at the skinny cop, still not fully recovered from the shock.

"Sir, would you like to go downstairs to see?" the skinny policeman said.

"Yes, goddammit, I would."

The skinny policeman escorted me down the stairs. A thought swept swiftly by my sleepy brain. That fucking Coach Harris is behind this. My poor Volkswagen was completely turned over. All four wheels were pointed up to the sky—just like the skinny policeman had said. There was graffiti writing all over the poor Bug.

"Damn!" I murmured.

"Sir?" the policeman answered.

"Nothing, Officer, just thinking out loud."

"Mr. Perez, do you have any idea who would do something like this?" the skinny policeman asked.

"No, Officer, just help me turn it over on all fours, would you?"

"Sorry, Mr. Perez, I can't help you, but I will call a wrecker for you. Sir, will you sign this report? Thank you."

What a jerk. Doesn't even want to help me. I am a damn taxpayer. These pigs just go around busting homeless people on the beach. Shit, I'll have to call the school and have someone cover my first-period class.

CHAPTER 3

Principal's Office

It took the wrecker seventy-five minutes to get to the apartment, and it took him five minutes to flip the car over. He took $100 from me. What a lousy morning!

Rushing back to school, I began to wonder why someone would pull such a stupid prank.

Could it be some gang members, or was it Coach Harris? He was big enough to flip it over. I have read articles about teachers having traumatic and psychological attacks by their student and peers. But why me?

I've always been dedicated to my profession. I've always tried to establish a meaningful relationship with my students, to help them strive to develop independence and self-reliance, so they could sustain their interest in education. Shit! Maybe I am just an idealist or maybe a fool.

I walked up the steps toward the corridor through Smoker's Alley. I felt a certain uneasiness watching the students laughing and running up and down the steps, grabbing one another's asses. The laughter echoed in the hallway as I entered the principal's office. I was greeted by Mr. Nguyen's secretary, Ms. Jimenez. She had a nice personality, very outgoing, but she was very ugly. She had a husky voice, a flat chest, and a flat ass, and she wore too much makeup. I am not mocking her. She has one good quality: she's a good person. That's more than I can say for most people, especially those around this school. There were rumors that she was having a love affair with one of the teachers from the English Department. How kinky! Ms. Stevenson handed me a message from Mr. Nguyen's desk. He wanted to see me as soon as I came in.

Ms. Jimenez smiled and winked mischievously at me. There was also a message in my box, a transfer for Chris to another history class. I was stunned at what they had done to me. It was Coach Harris who was behind all this, I decided.

Coach Harris and Mr. Nguyen were smoking and drinking coffee as I entered the office.

"Have a seat, Steve," Mr. Nguyen said with a smile—that stupid chameleon smile of his.

I guess I was his prey, and he was going to devour me. I felt uneasiness there with Coach Harris present. I felt my upper lip quiver.

"Good morning," I replied, knowing damn well I didn't mean it. As I seated myself next to the doorway, I could feel that they were up to something.

"What ever happened to you, Steve? Did you slip in the shower? Your face looks a mess. You should go see the school nurse."

I could see Mr. Nguyen smile. That creep. He knew good and well that Coach Harris had beaten me up.

"Thank you. I have already taken care of it."

"Oh, by the way, have you read your memo about Chris's transfer?" Mr. Nguyen asked.

"Yes, I did, and I don't like it," I replied angrily.

"It was necessary to avoid problems with the boy's parents. You can see that, can't you, Steve?"

I was ready to erupt like a volcano, but I managed to keep cool. I don't know how, but I did. The steam was coming out from both of my ears. I was ready to erupt violently, so I got up, threw the memo in the trashcan, and walked out. He continued talking to me as I was leaving. He advised me that if I persisted with my accusation about Coach Harris that there would be disciplinary actions taken by the school board. Also, he advised me to resolve our misunderstanding, saying it wasn't professional to continue such confrontations. He was still bitching when I closed the door behind me. Those unscrupulous jerks!

My ribs and lips were beginning to hurt. I stopped at the restroom to have a look at my disfigured face. The gall of that buffalo! He and the school board can kiss my neighbor's cat's black butt. Nevertheless, I stubbornly decided to continue my accusation to the school board. My lip was still swollen, and I stared in the mirror, examining the grotesque mass of flesh.

The day had gone rapidly. As usual, the students were incredibly uncontrollable but even more so today. I was in a precarious situation. Students are perceptive animals. They can sense the anxieties and bafflements of a teacher and take and use them for their own benefit. The word had spread like a range fire that I had a fistfight with Coach Harris and that I had gotten the worst end of the stick. The aftermath of the right cross was in plain view. I had the class read out of their library books that they had checked out, so I wouldn't have to talk too much. Each time I would say something, blood would trickle out. I used a whole roll of towel tissue on my wound. I could hear the students whispering to one another during class. They were talking about my disfigured lip. They even gave me several nicknames: Blood Alley Lip and, best of all, Monster Lip, among others.

CHAPTER 4

Funeral

Last week had been a long one. My so-called peers had alienated themselves from me. It was like I had the black plague. They didn't talk to me or eat with me in the cafeteria. They were giving me the silent treatment. I wondered if it would last through the remainder of the school year. God! I hope not.

The district game was lost on Friday night, 36-14. The team played badly: too many personal fouls, fumbling the ball too many times. Chris didn't play; he was benched. He had paced up and down the sideline with his head hanging very low. I felt like a heel, but nevertheless, it had to be done.

The Friday-night dance didn't have the usual spirit. The music was down-to-earth: Pearl Jam. I heard "Even Flow" about twenty different times. Not even the music picked up the pace. Most of the students were lingering around Smoker's Alley, smoking pot or just cracking on one another. My duty was to see that the students didn't get out of hand with their necking at the dance.

I had to talk with some of the members of the school board about drugs on the school grounds. They informed me that there would be a surprise search on Saturday morning through the students' lockers. It didn't go too well with the faculty. I didn't mind. Mr. Nguyen organized the search. Very much to his surprise, we found a big load of paraphernalia: ten bags of pot, roach clips made from metal-shop water pipes of all sizes and shapes, and even a bag of oregano. All were flushed down the toilet. Several students would be called in to Mr. Nguyen's office first thing in the morning on Monday. The search through the lockers was very invasive of the students' privacy. But it was a precaution. The parents were in favor of having a clean environment for learning.

The Saturday newspaper had a huge article on a former student who was killed in Iraq last week. I knew Johnny Martinez. He was an average student, very nice, and polite. Johnny had given his life to save a patrol that he was on. He had fallen on a grenade to protect his buddies. His body had received all the impact and shrapnel from the grenade. He was given a Silver Star posthumously, which was sent to his mother with a telegram. Johnny's body had come through the Fort Dix Army Terminal during the week. His mother and friends brought his body back. There were rumors that the coffin wouldn't be open because he was missing parts of his body.

The school board decided to let the student body go to the funeral. There would also be a ceremony for his mother in the auditorium. The superintendent would do the honors and dedicate a stadium in Johnny's name for his heroic action in Iraq. Johnny's mother would receive an eight-by-six mahogany plaque with an insignia bearing her boy's name. The plaque would hang in the new stadium's right corridor. The ceremony would be a short one so the students could go to the funeral.

"After roll call, class, we'll go to the auditorium, and I would like you to go in orderly fashion. I want the whole class to sit together. Do you understand? All together!" I said authoritatively.

These animals need some discipline. As usual, the students were delighted at not having class. Most weren't even aware of why we were going, just that it was a day off from school. Half the class made their way through the exits of the building toward Smoker's Alley to have a quick one.

Superintendent Stevenson walked up to the podium. Some of the local dignitaries and Councilman Green were to present the plaque to Mrs. Martinez. The local media was there to cover the ceremony. Stevenson cleared his throat to address his young audience.

"On a day like this, when one of our boys dies on the battlefield to stop communist aggression and to protect our way of life, I'm proud to call myself an American. I know how Mrs. Martinez feels today. She feels proud to have a son like Johnny who died for his country. Private Martinez was an outstanding citizen and a good American. He died to protect our freedom, which our young people take for granted. You young people today should be proud, as I am, that we have boys like Private Martinez in Iraq. He should be a model for you to follow."

Stevenson paused for a few seconds. His emotions were getting the best of him, or at least, it seemed that way. It was an election year, so the dignitaries gave Stevenson a standing ovation. It seemed that he was foaming from the mouth. I had never seen him like that, so melodramatic, so emotional. I knew he was a veteran of the Vietnam War and had a bad experience there, probably got the clap. But that was a long time ago. The students and staff were shocked at his emotionalism. Stevenson resumed his speech but decided to cut it short. "Here to present the award to Mrs. Martinez is our distinguished guest, Mayor Peabody."

The students all stood up and gave Superintendent Stevenson an enthusiastic standing ovation. Mayor Peabody unveiled the mahogany plaque and presented it to Mrs. Martinez. The media went wild with their cameras. The flashes blinded the student body and staff. Mayor Peabody was taking advantage of the media and began politicking for his next election, shaking hands with the staff and with some of his future voters.

Driving with the snakelike caravan from Saint James Catholic Church through the small community toward the cemetery, I still felt nausea from Stevenson's emotional eulogy. That pompous turkey! As the caravan arrived, the honor guard was smartly stationed by the open grave with rifles in hand. Most of the community was there to give

Johnny his last farewell. Even the veterans from foreign wars were there.

The priest began his eulogy, blessing the casket. One of the soldiers folded the flag that was over the coffin into a neat triangle and presented it to Mrs. Martinez, with a sharp salute. The bugler began to play taps. The shots echoed off the nearby mausoleums. It brought chills down my neck as it rang in my ears. Some of the older people had tears in their eyes. The younger generation stood in the background, laughing and joking around. The burial was short, a military one. The crowd began walking away from the new gravesite toward their cars.

CHAPTER 5

The Devil

51

I woke up with a scream. God! What a dream! My sheets were soaked with sweat. The horrible nightmare was about Johnny's funeral, but I was the one who was in the casket. I could see that parts of my body were missing. Coach Harris, Chris, and Vanessa were the pallbearers. I could see vividly that I was trying to get out of the coffin, but Coach Harris kept closing it. I could see that I was I screaming, blood pouring out of my body. I had pieces of flesh falling from my body. The group was dressed in black robes, and their faces were painted red.

Coach Harris was Lucifer. They were chanting over me, dancing, and drinking blood from golden goblets. I could see blood dripping from their mouths. They picked me up from the coffin and placed me in the middle of the pentagram. They began to dance around me, chanting. Coach Harris stood over me with his arms folded on his chest. Vanessa began to dance around me, holding a chicken with its head cut off. She then started to rub the blood all over her body.

As the rest started chanting louder and louder, I could see myself trying to crawl from the middle of the pentagram. I was like a worm with its head cut off. All my limbs were missing. Vanessa came toward me, then viciously began stabbing me all over my body. She had an unusual smile on her face. My god, what a dream!

It was like a Stephen King movie. Still in a pool of sweat, I got up and went to the bathroom to vomit. Taking a long warm shower would help me. Suddenly, a horrible thought came to mind: Anthony Perkins. He would pull the shower curtain and stab me with the knife he used on Janet Leigh. God! I had to get out of the shower to vomit again in the toilet bowl. I managed to empty my stomach of the remaining pizza and beer that I had last night.

Still thinking about the nightmare, the classroom door opened as I was correcting the students' homework. It was Coach Harris, with that diabolical smile on his face. I wanted to smash him in the face. I wanted to pay him back. But a fight would only bring about my dismissal. I made the obvious decision. I got up and faced the blackboard. Coach Harris moved his bulky body toward me and leaned his weight on me. *Wham!* He hit me with the back of his mammoth hand. I bounced from the blackboard. I felt the pain all the way to my toes. I found myself on the floor. The pain was unbelievable. Pain on the left side of my face sent flashes to my brain. My face ached. I saw Coach Harris leaving, and I managed to get up and sit in my chair. Tears began to flow down my eyes. What am I going to do about this son of a bitch? My face had puffed up a little, not very noticeable, but I was horrified. I felt nauseous. The door opened. They came in.

I managed to keep my composure all morning. In the middle of the day, I made some eye contact with Mr. Nguyen, but he ignored me. I never felt more depressed. I had the idea that I would get an ass kicking every day. But I still had to go on and get that asshole. I was determined to get even. I just had to. My job and my pride were at stake. Somehow, I had to persuade the staff and parents about Coach Harris. I had to fight back.

The empty school corridor was quiet and still. Debris from the candy wrappers was floating in the air. I felt depressed. I didn't even want to leave the school grounds. I was afraid to go to my apartment. It was still early. I had time to drive down the highway before the fog came in. Suddenly, the door opened from inside the school, and there stood the old janitor with a grin on his face. It was the first time I had seen him with a grin in five years.

"Hi," I said.

He said nothing, just shook the dust from the oily broom and walked back into the building. Some of the students were still leaving the parking lot.

I walked down the corridor toward Smoker's Alley to check if any of the students were still in the school area. I could still remember last year, when the students rushed into the principal's office to demand a smoking area. Their demand was obviously refused. It triggered a protest. The angry students, on their way out of the building, blew out all the toilet bowls from the west wing. They broke windows, and trashcans were set on fire. They assembled in front of the administration building. The police came immediately.

The walkout resulted in the arrest of thirty students on various charges, including inciting to riot, trespassing, vandalism, and possession of marijuana. The local police came in paddy wagons and with riot equipment. Several of the students were injured. The walkout lasted for three days. Several of the students were expelled for their subversive activities. Pressure from the community made the school trustees implement the smoking area for these little animals.

CHAPTER 6

Memories

I lay on my bed trying to forget the whole ordeal that was happening to me. I began to dwell on my childhood to keep my sanity. Could there have been some incident in my childhood that would cause me to become funny? My god! I had a normal childhood. But why am I so attracted to Chris? Could it be that I am going through latent homosexuality? Or could it be that I admire Chris for being a superstar? He has all the girls that I just dream about. I was born and raised in Refugio, Texas, one of the smallest towns in Southeast Texas, population 2,050. Historically, it's a Mexican town. Some fifty Texans defended the small Spanish mission from the Mexican dictator, Santa Anna. The result was disastrous for the Texans, as for the missions La Bahia and The Alamo.

My father ran off from his obligations, leaving five fatherless children and an alcoholic wife. What I vividly remember about my father is that he would come in late every Saturday night and beat my mother. He would find her drunk, and just like clockwork, he would be arrested for wife beating.

The only thing I really liked about my childhood was running through the woods and swimming in the oily Mission River. My brother and I had a hideout where we spent most of our time horsing around. There, we spent our time playing Tarzan. We had ropes on every oak tree down the riverbank. There, we would swing and dive into the river like Johnny Weissmuller would in order to save some damsel in distress.

Our African counterparts were three black kids from the neighborhood. Whenever my brothers needed an African uprising, we would invite them. They would paint their faces with white and yellow finger paint. We made African huts out of old corn stalks. After their huts were made, they would capture one of my younger brothers. We would run through the woods. They would follow with their wooden spears. The climax of the uprising would be when I would get on top of the largest oak tree and holler like Tarzan. Then my brothers would stampede the African wildlife, which consisted of a few cows and horses from the nearby pasture.

The woods were full of berries and wild life. Cottontails and quails were plentiful throughout the woods. My brothers and I would bring down a few of them with our slingshots. We thought we were the great white hunters with our primitive weapons.

As the years went by, I grew out of my gawky adolescence. I started working to help support the family at Old Man Martin's Fruit Stand. The fruit stand stood next to Highway 77. Mr. Martin was a crabby old fart who was half blind in one eye. A fruit crate had fallen on his head some years back. His right eye was damaged from the blow. Some of the kids called him One-Eye Jack because he wore a patch. He was strong for a man in his midsixties.

The biggest disappointment in my life was when Uncle Abe decided to draft me into the army. I spent my tour of duty in Fort Ord, California, with the Forty-First Infantry Battalion. I fell in love with Northern California, especially the Monterrey Peninsula and Highway 1. Never had I seen such scenic beauty in my life. I was discharged at Fort Ord and decided to continue my education at San

Jose State, where I received a baccalaureate of arts in secondary education.

As the evening fog came inland, so characteristic of Santa Cruz in the fall, the sweet aroma of the cool breeze swept by my nostrils, awakening me from my daydreaming. Tears rolled down my cheeks. The salty taste reminded me of Coach Harris. That jerk! I had to get him fired. I had to convince the school board and faculty. If only I could get one of the players to spill the beans to the school or the police. Loyalty! That stupid word. Loyalty! They worship him.

CHAPTER 7

Smoking

I t was an unexpectedly clear, humid morning as I awakened in the middle of my dream. Immediately, I jumped up and went to the bathroom to clean up. I felt good this morning. I had made a few calls last night to some of the board members. I had explained my situation with the school and my accusation about Coach Harris. They ranged from assault to the distribution of dangerous drugs. The members assured me that they would take positive steps to clear the matter up. They would have an inquiry on the allegations. But they said that I had to produce some type of evidence to back my story.

As usual, the biggest festivity was the pep rally in a game against an archrival. The anxiety of the students was phenomenal. Their spirits were up. Students were wearing the school colors and the football players their numbers. Even I felt the electricity flowing through me. I felt proud. Tonight, it would be up to them to lift the morale following the disastrous defeat of last week. The cheerleaders would use their best routines.

I still can remember, growing up, football was everything in my hometown, especially the Dallas Cowboys and the hometown team. There were big gambling deals made on what team would win, by how many points, and so on. Only the rich Irish would have money to make these types of wagers. My brothers and I would tag along with the boys. We would gather on the dark side of the stadium where we could go under the fence without being detected. Years back, the gang had made a hole large enough for two to crawl under it. We went in pairs in five-minute intervals. The first pair would signal by whistling that the path was clear. Most of the time, we didn't see the game. The boys started their own game on the side of the stadium. The remarkable thing about it was that we boys attracted more spectators when the hometown team was losing. Then the policemen would run us up to the bleachers and confiscate the cup stuffed with paper from the bathroom that we used as a football.

At the age of fourteen, I wasn't very interested in girls. I was still running with the younger boys, pulling childish pranks. But once, I got an opportunity to meet some girls with this Mexican boy named Joe. I still can remember the long shower that I took and the aftershave lotion Old Spice that I poured all over my body. I wanted to smell nice for the girls. But my mother had another idea, and she made me take another shower. She said I smelled like a walking French bordello.

Joe was a short skinny boy with a dark pimply face. Joe and I had made plans at school during lunch. That evening, we made our way to the *mercado* to buy some cigarillos. We were going to show the girls that we were puro macho. But the outcome of the cigarillos and Old Spice escapade wasn't too impressive. I got so damn sick from the small cigar that I never even made it to the restroom. I vomited twelve flights down the bleachers.

Today was a special day for the varsity squad. The squad would be presented with full honors for their athletic ability throughout the year. Some of the members would receive individual honors for their contribution to the game of football. Others would receive the school's letter. The squad was mostly made up of graduating seniors.

Chris O'Connor, obviously, would be the first to be introduced. Not that he needed it. It would be the third time he would receive the school letter. Also, he had been nominated for All-Around Athlete of the Year by the coaches of the school district.

Let's go, let's fight, let's win tonight!

Let's go! (clap, clap, clap)

Let's fight! (clap, clap, clap)

Let's win (clap, clap, clap)

Let's go, let's fight, let's win tonight

Let's go!

After the brief introduction of the squad, the cheerleaders ran out from the bleachers. They were jumping and tumbling on the track field. There was a short announcement that Vanessa Hempstead would not participate because of an upset stomach. It seemed queer that Vanessa wasn't going to be at the pep rally. She was usually the first to start the ball rolling. I've seen her jump around during a game with a broken leg that she got while skiing in Squaw Valley. And I knew some upset stomach wasn't going to keep her out. There was more to it. I got the feeling that something was wrong. I didn't even see her in the bleachers nor around the stadium. I thought I'd better go down to investigate. I made my way through the students, as the boys were whistling at the cheerleaders. I didn't blame them. The routine was very arousing.

I ran into Ms. Jimenez, standing by the gate. She was there to keep the students from skipping the pep rally.

"Hi, Mr. Perez." Ms. Jimenez said with a smile.

The woman was wearing a see-through blouse, no bra, and tight pants that made her skinny butt look a wee bit bigger.

"Hi, Ms. Jimenez, enjoying the pep rally?"

"Yes, it's marvelous."

"Ms. Jimenez, have you seen Vanessa?" I asked.

"Yes, I have. I saw her walking toward the field house a few minutes ago. Why?" she replied very suspiciously. She seemed puzzled by my concern for Vanessa. That overbearing witch. I can imagine what she was thinking.

Meanwhile, the pep rally was at full head of steam, the pom-pom girls were moving their balls of chrysanthemums over their heads and screaming in a ritualistic manner for blood. I made my way through the entrance of the field house, where the odor of sweaty dirty socks crashed against my nostrils. My eyes were becoming dilated from the strong fragrance. Damn, it's funky down here! I see why the players and coaches stay down here for only twenty minutes during the half. Any longer and it would kill you.

I manage to divert my attention from the smell and made my way through the dark hallway. It looked like a medieval dungeon. Coach Harris's office was small and cozy and surprisingly very neat. There were several pictures on the wall of him when he was at Stanford. Just the presence of the pictures brought chills down my neck. I felt very uncomfortable. My eyes began to scan the room. I noticed a book on his desk. It was a library book. It was one that I had recommended last week for a book report on Asia. I picked up the book and found out it had been hollowed out in the middle. How interesting. I began to look around for some evidence. Something that I could pin on him. The first aid kit—maybe there would be something. A syringe or pills. Damn, nothing. Just a bunch of tape and Band-Aids. I better get back to the pep rally.

The hollowed-out book was still rambling around in my mind. Why would someone do that to a book? It was a good way to hide drugs or a bag of pills. That's it! That's how Coach Harris brings his drugs in. I wonder if he sells them to the players. Let's see when the book was checked out. About three months ago. How ironic. There's a war halfway around the world and one right here between Coach Harris and me.

The afternoon had passed rapidly because of the pep rally. I kept pacing back and forth from my bedroom to the kitchen, wondering what to do. I decided that tonight, during the football game, I would get the police and members of the school board to question Coach Harris. There, they could make an insignificant bureaucratic decision, which would be the dismissal of one lousy coach.

Finally, I manage to sit down and turn on the tube before I wore out the carpet. Suddenly, there was a violent knock on my door. *Bang! Bang!* I jumped to my feet. What the hell was going on? *Bang! Bang!*

"Who is it?" I screamed.

"It's me, Mr. Perez. Chris! Chris O'Connor!

I opened the door all pissed off.

"What the hell do you want, Chris, and why aren't you at the stadium?" Chris looked pale and sickly. "What's wrong with you? Come in."

"Mr. Perez, Vanessa is dead."

"What!"

"She's dead!"

"Get a hold of yourself, Chris. Please repeat what you just told me. But slowly."

"They found Vanessa dead by the field house after the pep rally."

"Oh god, oh my god."

Chris was weeping like some baby who had lost his mother in some large shopping center.

"Get a hold of yourself. How do you know she's dead?"

"The ambulance and police are there. I heard someone say that Vanessa was dead. They didn't let me near the place where they found her. It's all my fault that Vanessa's dead. I introduced her to marijuana and barbiturates that we got from the coach."

"Shut up, Chris! Get yourself together, and we'll go to the school."

"No, I'm scared."

I felt sorry for Chris. He was inconsolable, and he blamed himself for Vanessa's death. If she was really dead, there would be many questions asked by the police, and I wanted to be there for Chris.

CHAPTER 8

Tragedy at School

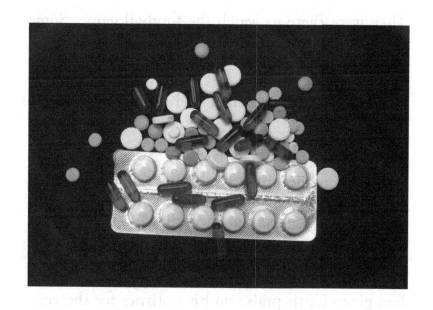

It was seven-thirty by the time we arrived at the stadium. Chris rode silently with his head hanging low. Within ten minutes of our arrival, cars were backed up, bumper to bumper. People had to get out and walk to the main gate because of the massive congestion of cars. Some of the fans didn't know what was going on, nor did I at this time. They were there to watch the football game. Some of the fans started chatting about the last time the two teams got together. It had been a great game. They expected no less this time.

As we made our way through the enthusiastic crowd, a few of the fans recognized Chris from his pictures in the sports section. The sports columnist had given Chris praise on his statistics for the year. His passing and touchdown stats were incredible for a high school senior. Chris was considered the top quarterback in the state. The sports columnist's analysis of Chris's four years was that he would be the most sought-after quarterback in the state by the top-ranked colleges in the nation.

"Give 'em hell, Chris!" one fan shouted out as we made our way toward the stadium.

We went through the back tunnel to avoid the crowd. The tunnel leads to the track field. There, as we came out into the light, people were running around like they had their heads chopped off. I seized one young girl by the arm and asked her what was happening. But some lady took her by the arm and gave me a nasty look. Some students were being helped out by hand, and others were carried out by stretchers. Police were everywhere. My god, it can't be true! My heart began to beat very rapidly. I looked at Chris. He was white as a sheet. His eyes were red. He had aged about ten years. I noticed that the cheerleaders were encircled by the police near the corner of the field house. Coach Harris and Ms. Jimenez were there too. Bewilderment showed in their eyes. I felt sick. A policeman approached me and gave me a soft shove with his nightstick.

"Sorry, sir, you'll have to move back."

"I'm a teacher here."

He looked toward Coach Harris for approval. He nodded. I rushed toward Ms. Jimenez. She stood there sobbing.

"What the hell is happening here?"

Still sobbing, she said, "They found Vanessa's body by the field house nude."

"Was she raped?"

"I don't know, Steve. All I do know is that they took her to the hospital to pump her stomach out.

They said she took some pills. They found her purse on the grass near the field house. It had a container with barbiturates."

I looked up at Coach Harris.

"That bastard did it!"

I leaped at Coach Harris, bringing up my right hand and catching him with a quick uppercut. The blow glanced off the side of his throat. Coach Harris stood motionless for a few seconds, not really feeling pain. I wanted to inflict more pain to his body, but within seconds, the skinny policeman grappled me down to the ground. His skinny arms tightened on the back of my neck. As I screamed at Coach Harris, "You son of a bitch, you killed her!" the policeman's arm tightened more around my neck.

"I will let you up if you behave, Mr. Perez," the skinny policeman said.

I was making such a scandalous scene. I was kicking and screaming at Coach Harris. That ridiculous scene brought more police to the aid of the strangler. The skinny cop kneed me in the back, which sent messages throughout my spinal cord. He twisted my arm back. The pain was sharp and to the point.

"Are you going to behave, sir? If not, I will take you downtown and book you."

"For what?" I screamed.

"For assault, to start with. Now, get yourself together and I will let you get up, okay?"

Ms. Jimenez looked at me with amazement and said, "How can you accuse Coach Harris of this?"

"Oh, shut up! You were so damn busy waiting for your lover—"

"Go to hell, you bastard!" she screamed at me.

"Knock it off, both of you!"

Coach Harris forced himself to stay away from me. He spoke from five feet away. "Where's Chris?"

I looked around, moving my head right to left and still feeling the pain that this bastard inflicted on my back. "He came with me. He must've gotten frightened."

I shoved the skinny asshole and began to run through the crowd that had assembled around us. Some of the women started screaming as I made my way through the crowd, knocking over some old fat lady. Behind me, I could hear the skinny policeman's footsteps pounding like a long-legged gazelle's, making tracks after me. I made it to the tunnel that lead to the parking lot that was packed with police cars. An impulse made me slow down when I ran into a black policeman. He looked at me for a moment—that steady glance that they give one when they are suspicious. Oh god, I hope he doesn't detain me. The gazelle is behind me.

"Hey, what the hell is wrong with you, running through the parking lot? Don't you know you can get hurt?" the young black policeman said.

"Yes, sir, but the students are having a riot in the stadium."

"Holy crap!"

The young policeman took off toward the tunnel, holding his .357 steady as it bounced up and down against the side of his leg. Boy, what a dumb jerk!

CHAPTER 9
Cruising

I swung out of the parking lot onto LaFonda Avenue, glancing at my rearview mirror, taking a second look to check if any black-and-whites were on my tail. My decision was not an easy one, but I needed Chris to put the finger on Coach Harris. My immediate concern was to find Chris before the police did. I made my reconnaissance along the main drag several times but no luck.

The sky had darkened, and the fog had intensified. I began to worry about Chris. I had to find him tonight; tomorrow would be too late for the both of us. His safety and my career were on the line. I made my way through the busy intersection of Water Street, where the students hung out on the weekends. I checked a few of the hamburger joints, not a trace of Chris. Where the hell could he have disappeared? There was no point in going to his home; he wouldn't be there. The police would check there first.

The only place I hadn't checked was under the Santa Cruz Boardwalk. As I made the illegal turn, I bounced off the curb, and I stepped on the accelerator, dodging cars to avoid a collision.

Santa Cruz Wharf had a long history of fatalities. During the last two years, the suicide rate among teenagers had risen 100 percent. Experts theorized that the increase of drug abuse had a lot to do with the phenomenon. I had visited the wharf a few times, and the view was spectacular. The feeling that I got when I was standing at the edge of the wharf was sensational. The beautiful rainbows were created by the sunlight and the mist; the tumbling rush of the waves on the rocks echoed in the large pylons off the wharf. The scenic beauty left me breathless.

The waves were like sirens that lured teenagers to their destruction. There was a small monument in memory of the first teenager who had leaped to his death. The boy was from somewhere in the Midwest.

The illumination from the cars blinded me momentarily. Then I noticed a lonely figure along the boardwalk as I passed near it on Murray Street. I couldn't tell if it was Chris. It could easily be some damn homeless veteran. But I decided I better make sure. I still had to go a quarter of a mile to the next exit. It took me a few minutes to find a place to turn around. I downshifted into second gear as I U-turned toward the entrance for the boardwalk. My Volkswagen began to backfire and smoke, then began to slow down. Poor devil, it'd taken hell these past years.

Sure as hell, it was Chris. He recognized me and started walking faster. I drove to his left side. He still kept moving. I shouted and opened the door, "Get your butt in, Chris!" Chris stubbornly continued walking. "Chris, please get in."

"Why don't you leave me alone?"

"Look, I'm trying to help you."

"Don't give me that bull, Mr. Perez!"

"C'mon, get in and we'll go back to my apartment, and we'll talk about it." I managed to convince Chris, and we started home.

The fog was so heavy; it was like a gigantic tidal wave. Every few feet, there would be a clearing and then *wham!* A heavy cloud would swallow my Volkswagen. I had never seen the fog this heavy before. I made the turn back to town. Chris glanced back and noticed two small lights that were cutting their way through the fog. The lights were getting much larger at a very rapid pace.

"I think someone is following us, Mr. Perez."

I glanced in the rearview mirror. Sure as hell, there was an automobile behind. I took a turnoff on Cliff Drive that led toward the beach. The lights that were following turned off too. There was an embankment that the surfers used to drive down on the beach. I headed toward it. Unmistakably, it was Coach Harris behind us. I recognized his dune buggy.

I drove up the embankment, a forty-five-degree angle, downshifting to second gear to get maximum acceleration. As I downshifted, my left hand stuck on the wheel. I was sweating nervously.

I was scared. Damn scared. Chris's baby-blue eyes seemed too much larger than usual. He was holding on to the seat like a small chimpanzee.

I don't know how my Bug made it to the top of the embankment; it was blowing smoke in all directions, farting and shaking the hell out of us. At one point, it seemed that we weren't moving. The rpm needle was jumping back and forth. I had the gas pedal to the floorboard. The old Bug just lost its stuff. Then, the beach was in front of us. I slam-shifted into third and kept my foot on the pedal. I never used my brakes, I didn't have to. They were shot. The sand would slow us down. So there was no need to worry. The immediate danger was behind us.

We were going down incredibly fast. When we got to the base of the embankment, the nose of my bug crunched, leaving the right fender twenty feet behind us. My foot was frozen to the pedal. If the old Bug did not let us down and did not stall on the sand, I swore to God, I'd give it a transplant.

There was sea drift and seaweed all over the beach. Some of the seaweed managed to entangle itself in the rear wheels. It was flip-flopping every which way, but I didn't let it bother me. I had my hands full zigzagging around the driftwood, smoking a few pieces with the right tire. With an unexpected *kabloom,* a huge spray of beach water was sent upward like a huge wave. My first reaction was to grab the steering wheel tighter and close my eyes. My god! I had run into the ocean! The windshield cleared to reveal that it was just a tidal pool that led into a large pylon. The old Bug stalled out on me. We need to get off the pylon. I could see

FRIDAY NIGHT FOOTBALL MURDER

the dune buggy's light a few hundred yards away. I grabbed Chris's arm.

"Let's get the hell out of here!" I shouted.

Chris jumped and slipped on some slimy green algae and fell on his butt.

"C'mon, move!" I screamed at him.

The water came up to our knees; it was damn cool. I reached back into the car. I opened the glove compartment to get my flashlight. I hoped and prayed my batteries were working. Chris and I began to move farther onto the pylons. The ocean seemed angry. The impact of its force pounded the boardwalk. The farther we moved under the boardwalk, the darker it got. I didn't dare use the flashlight until it was necessary.

"Chris, come out and I'll help you," Coach Harris yelled.

The echo sent chills down my back. "Don't you believe that garbage, Chris."

"But, Mr. Perez, Coach Harris isn't going to do anything to me. I am the star quarterback."

"My god, Chris, your girlfriend might be dead because of that lunatic! C'mon, move, he's right behind us." Now I had to use the flashlight. The darkness of the night was too much strain on the eyes. "Look, there's a large crevice. We'll hide in there."

"Mr. Perez, why don't you believe me? Coach Harris won't do anything."

"C'mon, let's get in there. He'll never find us. We'll stay until he leaves."

Minutes later, we got as comfortable as we could on the sharp edges of the rocks. The rocks were spearing our rumps. But there was not room enough to stretch our legs. The waves were beginning to fade from my mind. My god, what a night! I just couldn't believe that I could be in this unusual position—in some dark crevice, with a wet-nosed kid, the entrance blocked by some lunatic. Things had to get better.

CHAPTER 10

Kiss of Death

I woke up freezing. The wind was blowing fiercely, howling between the pylons. The tide was up. The water was splashing against my leg. My god, there was no way out! We were trapped like rats.

"Chris, move your butt before we drown!"

Chris got a kiss. *Smack!* A wave hit him with tremendous force, sending him onto his backside. I grabbed his arm before the swell swept him away.

"Are you okay, Chris?"

"Yes, what are we going to do?"

"Well, we're not going to stay here, that's for sure. We're going to swim like hell. That's what we're going to do. So pray like crazy, and get ready!"

"We're going to drown!"

"Shut up!"

Smack! A swell covered us with a fierce force. I managed to hold on to a hole in the crevice. My hand started slipping as the swell lifted me. I could feel the anger in the wave as the next one came and slapped me in the face.

Kabloom! The large swell covered us. I was holding as tight as I could to the rock.

"Okay, let's time the wave. Well, take a look at your watch!"

"It's not working!"

"Crap! Let's go."

We jumped into the water. It was waist high and very cold. Another wave was coming and looked even larger than the rest. The wave lifted us. I could feel the undercurrent sweeping me back. I managed to surface my head and get my balance on the base of the pylon.

"Look, Mr. Perez, there's your Volkswagen!"

The damn thing was floating right in the middle of the pylons. That lifted my spirits.

"Swim to it!" I shouted to Chris.

The current was taking its toll on my legs. I felt them giving up under its force.

I managed somehow to get to the old Bug. I was holding on to the fender, giving Chris a helping hand, one welcome to a very exhausted boy. The Bug was caught on some seaweed that managed to hold it in place. The Bug was rocking from side to side, which made it difficult to hold on to. The entrance of the boardwalk was about one hundred yards away. I was too tired to fight.

I manage to get to the door of the Bug and opened it. I jumped in to see if I had some dry

FRIDAY NIGHT FOOTBALL MURDER

clothes. No such luck. Not even a pair of dirty socks.

"Mr. Perez! Look, what's floating over there? It looks like Coach Harris!"

My god! I jumped in the water and moved toward the huge body of Coach Harris. He was floating facedown. I knew then that he was dead. I turned his body around. He had a huge cut on his forehead. His eyes were rolled back behind his sockets. He must have slipped on that green algae and hit his head and drowned last night. I tried to move his huge body, but something was holding his legs. They were wrapped around in the seaweed.

"Chris, come here and help me with Coach Harris. His legs are stuck in the seaweed."

Damn, he was heavy; his body had swelled up with the water he had in his lungs.

As much as I hated him, I felt like crying. And I felt sadness for Chris, who I knew worshipped Coach Harris.

"What are we going to do, Mr. Perez?"

"First, we have to get out of here and call the Highway Patrol. Chris, do you know a way out of here?"

"Just the way we came in. But what are we going to do about Coach Harris's body?"

"We can't carry him. We'll just leave him here. We'll call the police and tell them what happened. They'll know what to do."

The ocean breeze grew fresher and cleaner as we made our way to the boardwalk.

"Maybe we can wave a Smokey down, Mr. Perez."

"I hope so, Chris, I'm not young as I would like to be."

"You're doing okay for an old man."

"Haha."

"What's so funny, Mr. Perez?"

"Oh, nothing. Just that you have a traveling companion."

"What?"

"There's a starfish stuck to your ass."

The gas station attendant didn't notice us when we entered the office. He was dancing to some music from Tupac. The rhythm of his head and the snapping of his fingers were in sequence with the music. That is, if you call rap, music. He seemed to be in trance, his head bobbing with the sound of the song. The music was loud and not very soothing to my waterlogged ears. There was such a contrast to the sound of the ocean waves that I could still hear splashing against my eardrums.

The station attendant was a young black kid who had a huge natural and an iron comb stuck in it. He seemed to be out of the *House Party* movie.

"Yeah, dawg! What are you doing here? How come you're wet?" he asked.

"We took a midnight swim," Chris responded.

"You're shitting me, dawg! What wrong with you honkies? You're tripping. My boss don't like people who are loaded here," responded the black kid as he started combing his hair.

"Yeah right. Do you have a phone?" Chris asked.

"Say don't I know you? You're Chris O'Connor, the quarterback! What happened to the game last night? I heard last night that the game was postponed till next week. I can see why. You were out swimming in the damn ocean. Man, you're screwing up my bet. I got twenty-five on your arm to win by seven. So, man, don't screw with me up on my green. The phone's outside by the restrooms. Yeah, man, you got some weed on you?"

Chris looked at him and said, "I thought your boss didn't like people that were loaded."

"That's my boss but not me. I dig that shit. You have any marijuana or ecstasy?"

"No, dawg, I don't touch that stuff," Chris said with a guilty smile.

I pulled out a $5 bill from my wet wallet and handed it to the young attendant for some change. I made my way to the phone booth from where I would have to explain this nightmare to the police. The coffee that Chris bought was good. It was giving new life to my numb body. Black and strong.

I would need strength for the next few hours, not just for myself, but also for Chris. I deposited the 50¢ in the slot and dial 911 for the operator.

"Operator, this is an emergency. Would you contact the Highway Patrol for me? Thank you."

It didn't take the Highway Patrol and the Santa Cruz Police long to get to the scene. Moments later, the coroner arrived. They took us to the station of the Santa Cruz police for questioning. After a few hours, they released us, pending an inquiry into the death of Vanessa and Coach Harris.

The morning was beautiful, the sun burning through the fog. I felt like shit, sleepy and tired. I managed to get a yellow cab. The cabbie was a typical California hippie. He wore a large Hawaiian shirt and sneakers and drove like hell. He was rocketing down the street, blasting in and out through the residential neighborhoods. The streets were deserted, except for a newspaper boy pedaling his bike, trying to escape a Chihuahua, leaving newspapers scattered all over the sidewalk. The Chihuahua would momentarily stop and ravage one, then continue to pursue the biker. Within a few minutes, the cabbie stopped in front of my apartment. It was nice to be home.

"Did you hear the news last night? President Bush committed another twenty-five thousand troops to Iraq," the cabbie said.

"Damn, more boys are going to die," I answered.

Printed in the United States
By Bookmasters